Library of Congress Cataloging-in-Publication Data

McClelland, Julia.
    This baby / story by Julia McClelland; pictures by Ron Brooks. —
1st American ed.
        p.   cm.
        Summary: Andrew the bear sulks when he thinks about the new baby
that is coming to his family, until his parents tell him how much
they are going to need his help.
        ISBN 0-395-66613-9
        [1. Babies — Fiction. 2. Bears — Fiction.] I. Brooks, Ron, ill.
II. Title.
PZ7.M1319Th 1994
[E] — dc20   92-43756
                                                                  CIP
                                                                   AC

Text copyright © 1992 by Julia McClelland
Illustrations copyright © 1992 by Ron Brooks
First American edition 1994
Originally published in Australia in 1992 by Oxford
University Press

Printed in Hong Kong

10 9 8 7 6 5 4 3 2 1

5-91155

This Baby

Story by Julia McClelland

Pictures by Ron Brooks

Houghton Mifflin Company
Boston 1994

One day when Andrew went to sit on his mother's lap as usual, he noticed a strange thing. There was no longer any lap to sit on!

"Where has your lap gone, Mom?" he demanded.

His mother patted her large tummy.

"It will be back as soon as this baby is born — don't worry."

"But I *always* sit on your lap before bedtime," said Andrew. "This baby has taken *my* seat!"

His father scooped him up. "Come and sit with me instead," he suggested. But Andrew wriggled down again.

"I'm going to bed," he said. And he stomped off.

The next morning at breakfast Andrew said,
"This baby — can't we send it back?"

"It doesn't work like that," said his father.
"And anyhow, I'm sure you'll love this baby when it arrives."

"I'd rather we didn't keep calling it 'this baby,'" said his mother.
"Let's give it some sort of name."

Andrew thought about this.

"Is it a girl or a boy?" he asked.

"We don't know yet," answered his mother.

"Will it have any teeth?"

"Not straight away."

"Let's call it Gummy Face, then."

"That's not very nice, Andrew."

"Will it have any hair?"

"Not very much."

"Well, what about Baldy Head?"

Andrew's father took his son's hand.

"Come on, it's time for you to go to kindergarten."

At kindergarten, the children were asked to paint a picture of their families. Andrew painted his parents and then he put himself in between them, making the hands join up.

The teacher looked at his picture and said, "I'll bet you're looking forward to seeing the new little member of your family."

"No, I'm not," said Andrew.

"Why not?" asked the teacher.

"Because Mom and Dad have already got *me*. What do they want this baby for, anyhow?"

"So that you'll have someone to play with," answered the teacher.

"Oh," said Andrew.

When his mother came to get him, Andrew said,
"Will this baby be able to play tag with me?"

"Not for a couple of years," said his mother.
"Babies have to learn to walk before they can run."

"Babies sound boring," grumbled Andrew.

"*This* baby won't be boring!" said his mother. "Oh no, I called it
'this baby' again. Let's see if Dad has thought of a name yet."

Andrew's dad was in the nursery, painting the cradle.

Andrew was furious.

"That's *my* cradle!" he shouted.

His dad handed him the paintbrush. "Give me a hand, Toothy Face, and don't be silly. Only babies can fit into a cradle. You're a big boy with a proper bed."

Andrew threw the brush on the floor.

"I don't *want* to help and my name is not Toothy Face!"

Then he kicked over the paint can and made a dash for the door.

Before he could escape, his father grabbed him.
"Andrew! Just look at this mess! What on earth is going on?"

Andrew stood still, with his head down and his hands
in his pockets.

He sniffed loudly.

"Come on, Hairy Head," said his dad, "tell me what
the problem is."

"I don't *want* a baby around. It'll only break my toys and rip my
books and everything."

He sniffed again. "And there's all this stupid fuss over it."

"But a baby is worth fussing over," said his father.

"I bet you never fussed over *me* like that," said Andrew.

"We made even more fuss getting ready for you, Andrew.
You were our first baby. You are extra special."

"I don't remember you making any fuss over me," said Andrew.

"That's because you weren't born then," reminded his father.

"Oh, yeah," said Andrew.

But Andrew was still very cross. He was also bored.
He found his mother sitting in the living room with her feet up.

"Will you build a fort with me?" he asked.

His mother sighed. "Not right now, Andrew.
This baby is getting heavy, and I'm tired."

Andrew stamped his foot. "This stupid baby is wrecking
everything around here!"

His mother was shocked. "That's quite enough out of you, young man," she said. "You can go straight to your room and stay in there until your manners have improved."

"All right, I will!" Andrew bellowed at his mother. "I'll stay in there forever! I'll never come out! I'll *die* in there and then you'll be sorry!"

He slammed the living room door as hard as he could.

He slammed the bedroom door even harder.

Andrew was now so angry that he thought he would explode.

He kept thinking about a little crawling monster.

This monster had a hideous laugh. It went around smashing all his toys and chewing up all his books, laughing all the time.

Andrew jumped up and down on his bed shouting, "Go away! I don't *want* you here! Stupid baby — go away!"

When his parents came rushing in, they found Andrew lying
face down on the bed, sobbing loudly. Gently they turned him over,
sat him up and cuddled him until he stopped crying.

"Andrew, just listen for a minute," said his mom.
"We should have explained something to you. When you were born,
Daddy and I had to do everything ourselves. We had no one else
to help look after you, or play with you, or teach you."

His dad said, "This new little baby is incredibly lucky because it
will have *you* to be its friend. Imagine how the poor thing must feel,
coming into a strange world, not knowing what's going on."

Andrew stopped sniffing. He tried to imagine what it would be like to be a baby. What if you couldn't walk and couldn't talk and couldn't feed yourself when you were hungry?

"If it gets a cold," said his mom, "it can't even blow its own nose. It has to *learn* how to do everything that you can do. This baby needs you, Andrew. Please say you'll help it."

Andrew forgot about the monster. He imagined instead a small, helpless version of himself, lying in the cradle. Maybe this baby felt as angry and as bored as he did sometimes.

"I don't think it's much fun being a baby," he said.

A few days later, Andrew's mom asked, "Have you decided on a name for this baby until it's born?"

"Yes, I'm going to call it Learnalot because that's what it has to do."

"That's a good name," said his mom. "I want to knit a little blanket for the carriage. What color do you think Learnalot would like best?"

"Oh, Learnalot likes lots of colors," said Andrew. "You'd better make it red and blue and green and yellow with a bit of purple and orange."

"Right," said his mom.

Andrew's dad had finished getting the nursery ready.

"Well, that's it. Can you think of anything else?"

Without a word, Andrew went out. When he came back, he was carrying a small and rather worn blanket. He put it in the cradle.

His father was surprised.

"But Andrew — your blanket!"

"Learnalot can have it now."

The next time Andrew was at kindergarten, he painted a new
picture of his family. He put himself in between his parents, as usual,
but then he added a big round baby wearing a diaper.

At day's end, Andrew was surprised to see his Auntie Robyn.
"Where's my mom?" he asked.

"She's gone to the hospital to have the baby," said his aunt.
"And Dad's gone with her. I'm afraid you'll have to put up with me."

"It's a good thing I did this painting today, then," said Andrew. "I can give it to Learnalot."

Auntie Robyn looked at the picture and smiled. "I can see you're going to make a great brother for this baby," she said.

"Not 'this baby,' Learnalot," said Andrew.

"I beg your pardon?" said his aunt.

When Andrew and his aunt arrived at the hospital,
a nurse came to tell them that the baby had been born.

"Congratulations! You have a baby sister."

She showed them into a small, sunny room, where his mother
lay in bed holding the baby.

Andrew tiptoed to the bedside and stared at his new sister. She
was very small.

Her eyes were screwed up, her cheeks were bright red and her nose was squashed flat.

Andrew felt sorry for anyone who came into the world looking like that.

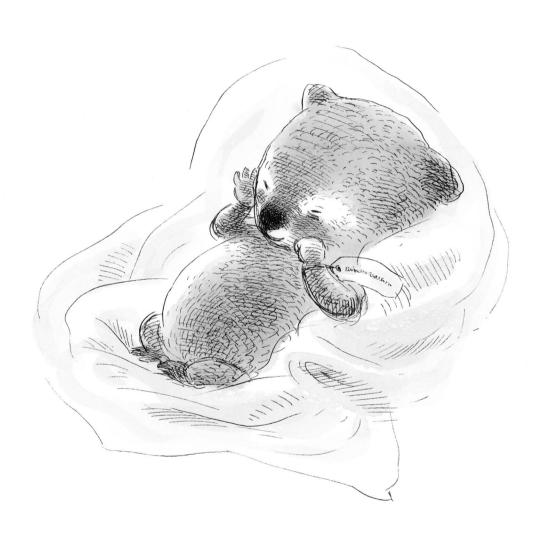

As he looked more closely, Andrew noticed that the baby was wearing a tag on her wrist.

"What's that?" he asked his mom.

"It's a message — for you," said his mom.

"For *me!*" said Andrew. "What does it say?"

Andrew's dad looked at the tag and pointed to the words as he read them. "Hi, Andrew. My name is Jane."

Then he turned the tag over and read the other side . . .

"But you can call me Learnalot."